GIRLS SURVIVE

Girls Survive is published by Stone Arch Books, an imprint of Capstone.
1710 Roe Crest Drive
North Mankato, Minnesota 56003
www.capstonepub.com

Library of Congress Cataloging-in-Publication Data

Library of Congress Cataloging-in-Publication Data Names: Smith, Nikki Shannon, 1971- author. | Trunfio, Alessia, 1990- illustrator. Title: Sarah journeys west : an Oregon Trail survival story / by Nikki Shannon Smith ; illustrated by Alessia Trunfio. Other titles: Girls survive. Description: North Mankato, Minnesota : Stone Arch Books, a Capstone imprint, 2020. | Series: Girls survive | Audience: Ages 8-12. | Summary: In 1851 twelve-year-old Sarah is a free Black, happy living with her parents, grandparents, and brother on their own farm in Iowa; but her father has been bitten by the gold bug and wants to take the trail west to California, and after some argument it is decided that the the grandparents will stay on the farm, but the rest of the family will go; the journey will be difficult and dangerous, but if they survive extreme weather, difficult terrain, illness, and the racism of others in the group there may be a better life waiting for them at the end of the trail. Includes nonfiction material on the Oregon Trail, a glossary, discussion questions, and writing prompts. Identifiers: LCCN 2019048260 (print) | LCCN 2019048261 (ebook) | ISBN 9781496587183 (hardcover) | ISBN 9781496592187 (paperback) | ISBN 9781496587190 (adobe pdf) Subjects: LCSH: African American families—Juvenile fiction. | Overland journeys to the Pacific—Juvenile fiction. | Frontier and pioneer life—West (U.S.)—Juvenile fiction. | Survival—Juvenile fiction. | Oregon National Historic Trail—Juvenile fiction. | California—Gold discoveries—Juvenile fiction. | West (U.S.)—History—1848-1860—Juvenile fiction. | CYAC: African Americans—Fiction. | Overland journeys to the Pacific—Fiction. | Frontier and pioneer life—West (U.S.)--Fiction. | Survival—Fiction. | Family life—West (U.S.)—Fiction. | Oregon National Historic Trail—Fiction. | California—Gold discoveries—Fiction. | West (U.S.)—History—1848-1860—Fiction. | LCGFT: Historical fiction. Classification: LCC PZ7.S6566 Sar 2020 (print) | LCC PZ7. S6566 (ebook) | DDC 813.6 [Fic]—dc23 LC record available at https://lccn.loc.gov/2019048260 LC ebook record available at https://lccn.loc.gov/2019048261

Image Credits
Capstone, 111; Shutterstock: kaokiemonkey, (pattern) design element throughout, Spalnic, (paper) design element throughout; AFBPhotography: Alan Bradley, 112

Designers: Cynthia Della-Rovere and Charmaine Whitman

Printed in the United States 4661

SARAH JOURNEYS WEST

An Oregon Trail Survival Story

by Nikki Shannon Smith

illustrated by Alessia Trunfio

STONE ARCH BOOKS
a capstone imprint

CHAPTER ONE

Montgomery County, Iowa
April 21, 1851

We always ate dinner together—me, Mama, Daddy, Granny, Granddaddy, and James. I liked that we all lived together. Mama and Granny loved to talk, and I was never bored or lonely. If I was quiet, sometimes they'd let me listen to things I wasn't really supposed to hear.

Mama was at the stove. "Did you hear the Tuckers are heading west?" she asked Granny.

"Sure did." Granny sighed and said, "So many folks running to California. That gold fever is something else—everybody trying to get rich."

Granny set a bowl of carrots on the dinner table. I couldn't tell if she thought making the trip west was a good idea or a bad idea. All I cared about was that we all lived under the same roof, and everybody was free. Some people didn't have it that good.

"I tell you what," said Mama. "I don't think the Oregon Trail is worth the risk. A lot of people die on that trail."

Just then, Granddaddy, Daddy, and James came into the kitchen. They walked in order from oldest to youngest, all of them dirty from tending our crops. Granddaddy was tall and thin, and Daddy was just a little shorter than his father. James was almost as tall as Daddy, even though he was only fourteen. He was always saying he was going to pass Daddy up one day.

"Smells good in here," said Daddy. He gave Mama a kiss on the forehead, then kissed Granny on the cheek. He gave me a big squeeze and said, "How's my Sarah?"

"Fine," I said.

"Go on and wash up," said Mama. "Food's almost ready."

A lot of our food came from our own farm. At least the eggs and vegetables did. Daddy didn't want to raise animals for meat. Sometimes he raised hogs and sold them, but he said he didn't have the heart to kill them. So when we had meat, it came from the farm down the road. Tonight, potatoes, carrots, and a bit of pork sat steaming on the table.

Once everyone sat with plates heaped up high, Daddy said, "The Tuckers are leaving for California."

"It's just foolish," said Mama. "They all goin'?"

Daddy shook his head. "It'll just be Henry and the oldest boy, Charlie. Henry doesn't want his wife and the younger kids making a trip like that."

I saw a flash in Mama's eyes, but it was

gone just as fast as it came. Mama couldn't stand for anybody to say that a woman shouldn't do something just because she was a woman.

I wondered what the trail was like. Sometimes when we went to town to shop, I overheard people talking about it. None of them had ever gone west, though. They had only heard stories. In most of the stories, somebody died, or got lost, or went too slow and got caught in the snow. I'd heard a couple of stories about people who turned around halfway there and went back home.

Finally Mama said, "Well, I'm glad we're here making a decent living."

Granny nodded. "Mmm hmmm," she said. "We have land and a home big enough for all of us. Plus, we have enough money from selling crops and eggs and doing odd jobs for people. Can't ask for anything more."

"Yes, we could!" exclaimed James. "We could

ask for *gold.* And lots of it. They say it's just sitting in the river waiting for you."

Granddaddy laughed. "Boy, you wouldn't last one day mining for gold. You already complain working in the field, and you don't have to stand in ice-cold water all day to harvest potatoes."

It was true. James did complain. I could still tell he liked being with Daddy and Granddaddy, though. He always stood up extra tall when he walked next to them.

"I heard it takes six whole months to get to California," I said.

Granddaddy took another spoonful of potatoes. "If you're lucky," he said.

The kitchen got quiet while everyone chewed. I figured we were all thinking about gold and California and people going west. I looked at Daddy and realized he hadn't said one word since we started eating. Sometimes Daddy was tired at the end of the day, but he didn't look tired. He looked like he was thinking. He stared down at his plate.

James broke the silence, as usual. "I want to get a job in town," he said, "at the general store."

"James, how are you going to do that?" Mama asked. "You have school and you have your chores here. You don't need a job anyway."

I had a feeling James wouldn't go to school if he didn't have to. He didn't care about reading or

math. James cared about money. We were opposites. I loved school.

"No," said Daddy. "You won't be getting a job."

Mama and Granny nodded in agreement. James frowned. Granddaddy minded his own business, which was what he usually did.

"Why?" asked James.

"Because," said Daddy, "you and I are heading west on the Oregon Trail with Henry Tucker."

CHAPTER TWO

Montgomery County, Iowa
April 21, 1851

I could tell right away Daddy was serious. It wasn't a joke. Mama took a breath so deep it sounded like she was trying to suck all the air out of the kitchen. Granny put her fork down and stared at her only son for a long time.

Nobody knew what to say. The kitchen was quiet, and it was quiet outside too. It was like all the birds were holding their breath waiting to see what would happen next. The longer we all waited, the more upset I got.

Daddy had made this decision all by himself. He hadn't talked to Mama or anyone else about this idea. He hadn't asked us if we'd be okay without him, or if we wanted to come. He hadn't thought about his own parents. He just decided to break up our whole family. I didn't want Daddy and James to leave.

I was afraid to be the first one to speak, so I sat at the table with a lump of potatoes in my throat and looked from face to face. Not a single face looked happy. Not even James's. He stared at Mama, who had a single tear rolling down her cheek.

Everyone started talking at the same time.

Mama said, "You can't just up and leave us, Theo."

"Dad, are you serious?" asked James.

"We just finished saying we have everything we need right here," said Granny.

"Then we're coming with you," said Mama.

Daddy pounded his fist on the table. "That's enough," he said. "The decision is made. Ada, you all are staying right here. This is no journey for women or twelve-year-old girls. It's too dangerous."

Most of the time, Daddy acted like he thought women should be equal, but when it came to safety, Daddy was in favor of the men doing the dangerous work.

"This doesn't have anything to do with being a woman," said Mama. "And if it's so dangerous, then maybe you need to stay put."

Granny pushed her plate away from her. I didn't know what to do, so I took her plate and mine to the sink. I didn't have an appetite anymore.

I hadn't asked to be excused, so I sat back down and looked at my brother. For once, he seemed speechless. He sat up straight with his head cocked to one side. He had gone from scared to proud in five minutes.

I was stuck on one feeling—mad. Everything about this made me mad: not being part of the decision, not being allowed to go, not having my family together anymore. The thing that made me madder than anything was that I didn't understand why.

"Why are you doing this to us, Daddy?" I had to work hard not to yell.

"Son, why *do* you want to do this?" asked Granny in a soft voice.

Daddy wiped his mouth and took a deep breath. He opened his mouth to say something, and then closed it again.

We all waited for his answer.

Finally he said, "We can have a better life. We can have more. I don't want the children stuck in Iowa their whole lives. I want them to have choices."

"There's nothing wrong with this life," said Mama. "Not one thing."

"But, Ada," said Daddy, "people are striking it rich. And they say there's more opportunity in California for Negroes. Think of what the children's lives could be like if I come back with that kind of money."

Granddaddy shook his head. "He's gon' do what he's gon' do. His mind is made up."

Mama stood up and looked down at everyone. "Then we'll all go."

"I'm not going," said Granny. "I'm just fine right here."

"Me too," said Granddaddy. Granddaddy loved *home*. Granny said he had built it from the ground up all by himself. She said over the years he'd added on to it so his whole family could be together.

Granny liked to say that they baked us up a life from scratch.

"Don't make me say it again, Ada. This is a man's journey." Daddy's voice was firm.

Mama started clearing the table. She walked back and forth, carrying one plate at a time. I had never seen Mama this mad. She looked like she wanted to throw a plate. Her lips were pressed closed, and she wouldn't look directly at any of us. When she ran out of dishes, she stood at the sink with her back to us. Even though Mama's anger made me nervous, Daddy deserved it.

"I remember a different journey," said Granny.

I knew what journey she was talking about. Sometimes, when it was just the two of us, she talked about it. Granny had escaped slavery. She said she'd lived in a horrible place. It was so bad she still got tears in her eyes every time she thought about it. She didn't tell me what happened there, just that one day she knew for sure she had to leave.

She was already pregnant with Daddy, and she said no baby of hers was growing up the way she did. She convinced Granddaddy and two of her cousins to leave with her. One night, they all ran away. They didn't even know where they were going. They ran in the dark and hid during the day. Granny and Granddaddy had made it to safety, but her cousins hadn't.

"My journey," said Granny, "was much more dangerous than this one."

We didn't dare interrupt Granny. Even Daddy stayed quiet. Mama faced us and leaned on the counter. I think if it wasn't for the counter, Mama might have collapsed.

"I wasn't trying to get rich," Granny continued. "I was trying to stay alive. I was keeping my family *together.*"

Granddaddy wiped a hand across his eyes and stood up. Without a word, he left the kitchen. I heard the front door open and close. I knew he would sit in the rocking chair on the porch. He sat there some nights and rocked for a long time. I always wondered what he thought about when he was out there.

I had a feeling I knew what he'd think about tonight.

"I knew one thing for sure." Granny lifted one finger and shook it at Daddy. "No baby of mine was going to be a slave. I didn't care about the risks. I was determined, and I made it."

Granny walked over to Mama and took her hand. "A woman can do anything a man can do, Theo. Anything."

I left the table and stood with the women. Daddy and James sat at the table alone, just like they'd be on the Oregon Trail.

Finally Daddy said, "James, Sarah, get ready for bed."

In my room, I slipped into my nightgown and sat on the bed. I wrapped myself in the quilt Granny made for me when I was a baby. It was faded and worn now, but it used to be bright green. The doll Granny made me for my fifth birthday sat on my pillow. I reached out and picked her up. My doll and I huddled under my blanket, and I tried to hear the whispers from the kitchen.

No matter what, we'd be separated, because Granny and Granddaddy refused to go anywhere. I didn't want to leave them. I didn't want to leave home. But I also didn't want to be without Daddy. I'd even miss James if they left.

I tried to make sense out of something I just couldn't understand at all. *I don't even want a different life,* I thought. I wondered if I'd be mad at Daddy forever.

I woke up early the next morning to what sounded like a lot of people in the kitchen. I walked in to find everybody already awake. Mama was taking some biscuits out of a skillet. James sat at the table like he was starving, and Granddaddy quietly sipped his coffee. Daddy was putting things from Granddaddy's homemade cabinets into a crate.

Granny noticed me standing in the doorway and said, "Good morning, baby."

Usually, Granddaddy and Mama were the only ones in the kitchen when I got up. Mama was always at the stove making breakfast, and Granddaddy was always at the table with his coffee. Most of the time they seemed to enjoy the silence.

"Why is everybody up?" I asked.

Granny walked over and wrapped her arms around me. "They made a decision. You're leaving," she said.

CHAPTER THREE

Montgomery County, Iowa
April 22, 1851

I couldn't believe my ears. I pulled away from Granny. "Leaving?"

"For California," said Granny.

Granddaddy set his mug on the table a little bit too hard. Daddy kept on packing the crate like we weren't in the same room. Mama set the biscuits on the table and sat down. I looked at my brother, who grinned at me. I did not smile back.

"Granny, are you coming?" I asked.

She shook her head and looked away.

"Granddaddy?" I asked. "Are you?"

Granddaddy twisted his mouth. "No, I am not," he said.

Daddy interrupted. "It's going to be you, James, me, and your mama."

"I don't want to go!" I said. "I like it here. I don't want to leave Granny and Granddaddy."

"Your daddy has it all planned out," said Mama. I looked into her eyes, but I couldn't tell how she felt about it.

"Why are *we* going?" I asked. "Daddy said we couldn't."

Daddy looked proud. "I realized this way we can stay together *and* you can have new opportunities even sooner. I have almost everything packed in the wagon out back. I've been buying supplies and saving money. Henry Tucker took care of the details. What we don't have we'll get at the jumping off point."

I didn't even know what Daddy was talking about. My family sat there like it was no big deal. We were leaving everything we had. We were leaving home and part of our family. "What about Granny and Granddaddy?" I asked.

"We'll send for them when we get settled," said Daddy.

Granny smacked her lips. "Oh no you won't. I'm staying right here."

Granny had a way of ending a conversation, so nobody bothered to answer. We ate breakfast in complete silence. James could barely sit still, and Mama sat so still she looked like a statue.

As soon as Daddy finished his food he said, "Well, we need to get going."

"Right now?" I asked. I hadn't packed anything or said goodbye to my friends. I realized then that Daddy had been planning to leave today all along, and he was never going to give us any warning.

He had waited until last night to tell us to make it easier on himself, but it didn't work.

Granny disappeared and returned with my doll. "Sarah, take her with you. She'll be good company, and you can tell her all your secrets."

I burst into tears. Granny hugged me and rocked back and forth. "It's gon' be okay," she whispered over and over again.

But it wasn't going to be okay. We were saying goodbye—maybe forever. We might not even make it to California. Anything could happen on the trail. If we did make it, I wasn't sure we'd ever come back to Iowa.

Daddy said, "Ada, you have all the clothes and food packed?"

Mama nodded. She stood in the middle of the kitchen and looked around. James stood next to Daddy with his hands in his pockets. Before I knew it, all six of us stood tangled in each other's arms in the middle of the kitchen. We stayed like that for a long time. I don't think anyone wanted to be first to break loose from our last hug.

Daddy finally let go and headed outside, followed by James. I ran to my room and grabbed my quilt. While I was in there, I noticed someone had come in during the night and taken some of my things. It must've been Mama, but I hadn't even heard her. I took one last look at my room, the same way Mama looked at the kitchen. New tears tried to come, but I blinked them away.

I was the last one in the wagon. Granny stood next to us, shading her eyes from the sun. Granddaddy had one hand on Granny's shoulder, and the other was holding a gun. Before Daddy got the horses going, Granddaddy handed him a roll of money. "You take this," he said. "It'll come in handy."

"I can't take that money," said Daddy.

Before Daddy could say any more, Granddaddy put a hand up to stop him. "Yes, you can. You will."

Then Granddaddy handed the gun to James. "James, you're going to need this to hunt. I pray that's all you'll need it for."

James grinned like a fool, but Mama hung her head and picked at her fingernails.

"I love you, Granny and Granddaddy," I said. "I'll write to you."

Granny gave me a sad little smile, and we were off to Kanesville, our first stop.

Kanesville, Iowa
April 29, 1851

After a week of bouncing around in the wagon, feeling homesick and lonely, and listening to James talk about hunting, I was excited when I noticed wagons in the distance.

"Daddy, are we almost at Kanesville?" I asked.

Daddy nodded. "Sure are. Our jumping off point is just ahead."

"What's a jumping off point anyway?" I asked.

"It's a gathering spot," said Daddy. "People meet up with their party, get their wagons ready to go, and then the real journey begins." Daddy pulled the wagon over to the side, near a farm with several oxen in a field.

"Why are we stopping?" asked James. "Everyone else is heading that way." He pointed ahead of us.

"This is where Henry said we should wait," said Daddy. He jumped down from the wagon, and we all followed. I was glad to stretch my legs and get off my sore behind. We stood in some grass on the side of the road and ate bread and dried pork. I watched a few wagons pass by and wondered how the people riding in them felt about leaving home.

After a while, Mr. Tucker's wagon arrived. He and Daddy shook hands and unhitched the horses.

"Daddy, what are you doing with the horses?" I asked.

"I have somebody taking them back to Granddaddy," he said. "We'll have some oxen to pull us."

I was glad he wasn't selling the horses. I watched as Daddy and Mr. Tucker took the horses into the field. They spoke with a man wearing dirty clothes and a hat. I could tell Mr. Tucker knew him. Before long, we had four oxen hitched to our wagon.

Four more wagons approached with oxen already hitched. "There they are," said Mr. Tucker.

They stopped next to us. The other wagons had six oxen instead of four, and all their drivers were white. Daddy, James, Mr. Tucker, and his son, Charlie, walked over to the second wagon. The passengers were a man, his wife, and two children.

One was a little boy. The girl looked about twelve years old, just like me. I smiled at her, and she smiled back. I hoped she was coming too.

The driver climbed down and shook Mr. Tucker's hand. "Mr. Lee," said Mr. Tucker, "this is Theo Lewis." Mr. Lee and Daddy shook hands.

The rest of the men climbed out of their wagons and introduced themselves. A man named Mr. Adams was the only one who didn't shake Daddy's and Mr. Tucker's hands. I hoped he wasn't about to spend the next six months hating us for being Negro.

Even though there was no slavery in Iowa, we got treated different all the time. James and I couldn't go to school with the white kids. There was a Negro lady Granny's age who ran a school out of her barn. That's where we went. Sometimes when we went to the store, white people gave us mean looks, and other times they avoided looking at us at all. Mr. Adams seemed like one of those kinds of people.

"Well, let's go ahead and vote for a captain," said Mr. Lee. "Who wants the job?"

Mr. Adams stepped forward. "I can be the captain," he said. "I have a map, a lot of hunting experience, and I'm strong." He puffed out his chest like he was trying to prove it.

Mr. Lee said, "I'm willing to be the captain too, since I pulled this group together."

"Well, let's vote and get going," said a tall, thin man called Mr. Edwards. He was traveling with another man who looked a lot like him.

Mr. Lee asked Daddy, "How old is James?"

"Fourteen. Why?" Daddy answered.

"Fourteen is old enough to vote," said Mr. Tucker.

Mr. Adams butted in. "Negroes can't vote."

Mr. Lee glared at him. "We aren't the Iowa

government. This is a group of people spending the next six months together. All men vote."

Everyone but Mr. Adams nodded.

I couldn't believe Mr. Lee had called James a man. Now he was going to start thinking he was a man and get on my nerves. There were nine men altogether, since Charlie was a year or two older than James.

"Well, vote then," said Mr. Adams.

Daddy, James, Mr. Tucker, and Charlie voted for Mr. Lee. Mr. Edwards, his brother Young Mr. Edwards, and a man who had his wife and an older lady with him voted for Mr. Adams. I was glad he lost, but something on Mr. Adams's face told me we hadn't heard the last from him.

"You can ride in your wagons for now," said Mr. Lee, "but after we cross the Missouri River, we'll walk. We don't want the wagons too heavy."

Everyone climbed back into their wagons.

"We have to cross a river?" I whispered to Mama. Things just kept getting worse.

She nodded. "This won't be an easy trip, but at least we're together."

All the wagons fell into a line behind Mr. Lee's. As we slowly rode into Kanesville, the crowd got thicker. People worked on wagons, bought supplies, and some were trying to get rid of things that wouldn't fit in their wagons. Men stood in the middle of the road looking at maps and books.

That wasn't all. There were women and children, and they were just as busy as the men. Women carried sacks of flour and little medicine bags. One woman was fixing a wagon wheel. I remembered Granny's words and knew she was right. *A woman can do anything a man can do.*

Soon our wagons came to a complete stop. In front of us were at least fifty wagons just sitting there—all waiting to cross the river. A young man sat in the back of his wagon playing the fiddle. Children rested in the shade of their wagons, and off to the side, two men with worried faces talked.

"The current is too strong," said the bigger man. "Maybe we should wait."

His friend said, "If we wait, we might not get there before winter."

The first man shook his head. "You saw what happened. That river claimed *two* oxen today."

I looked at Mama. "What does that mean?" I asked.

She took my hand. "The river is so fast it pulled the oxen and they drowned."

"But nothing bad will happen to us, right Mama?" I asked.

Mama didn't answer me.

We sat in silence. And the wide river spread out ahead of us like it was daring us to try to cross.

CHAPTER FOUR

Kanesville, Iowa
April 30, 1851

Our turn to cross the river didn't come until the next day. Mr. Adams and the Edwards brothers went first. I watched them unhitch their oxen. They carefully rolled their wagons onto a flat boat. The animals were tied with ropes so they wouldn't be swept away by the current as they swam across. After some arguing, Young Mr. Edwards got into the river with the animals. It seemed like a bad idea.

The boat headed across the river with Young Mr. Edwards and the oxen behind it. The boat kept getting caught in the current, and the man in charge of the boat kept yelling at Mr. Edwards and Mr. Adams to use the oars and poles to keep the boat straight.

"Mama," I whispered, "are they gon' make it?"

Mama shook her head and shrugged at the same time.

An invisible current snatched one of the oxen and dragged it downriver. I gasped and held my breath. Young Mr. Edwards couldn't catch it. The ox fought its way to the other side. Some people who had already crossed waded in, caught the rope tied to the ox, and pulled it to shore. Finally the boat unloaded its passengers and came back for us. The closer it got, the tighter the knot in my stomach twisted. I couldn't swim, and I didn't like the water. I was sure I didn't like boats either.

Daddy and Mr. Tucker had the oxen ready. Mama, James, Charlie, and I stepped onto the boat. I grabbed Mama's hand to keep my balance as the boat rocked. James looked at Daddy, and Daddy gave him a nod. I knew what that meant: Daddy was getting in. Once the wagons were on board, Daddy and Mr. Tucker stepped into the river with the oxen.

We were on our way. I looked back at Mr. Lee's daughter, who waited at the river's edge for her family's turn. She smiled and waved. Mama and I held on to each other as the boat turned and dipped. I was a lot smaller than an ox, so if I fell in and got pulled by the current, I'd probably drown.

I jumped when the man in charge yelled, "Ho! Steer!"

James and Charlie did their best to keep the boat headed in the right direction. James had a serious look on his face. He knew our lives were in his hands. I wondered how he felt about being a man now.

I looked down at Daddy swimming in the river. The river had gotten too deep to walk. I wanted to yell, *Be careful, Daddy,* but I didn't want to distract him. He already looked like he was struggling. Mama's eyes were wide with fear.

Finally I focused on the girl. She smiled and waved the whole time. No matter which way the boat turned, I kept her in sight. She was the only thing that kept me calm.

I didn't know we had made it across until James gave me a little shove. "Sarah, are you staying here forever?" he asked.

"No," I said and hurried off the boat. Daddy and Mr. Tucker led the oxen onto the shore. I counted them. Our four and Mr. Tucker's four were all there. It felt like a miracle.

After we all crossed the Missouri, we walked along next to our wagons until dusk. We weren't in

Iowa anymore. I wasn't sure where we were, but we were on the trail.

The order was Mr. Lee's wagon, then Mr. Adams's wagon, then the Edwards brothers'. We were fourth. Mr. Tucker was right behind us. The family of three was last in line. The man and his wife looked about the same age as Mama and Daddy. I thought the old woman was probably the man's mother. She rode in the wagon all day. A few times I looked back at her, and she always had a sad look on her face.

After a while I said, "Mama, can I go meet Mr. Lee's daughter?"

Mama shook her head. "No, I want you right here with me."

Since I couldn't go anywhere, I watched James act like he was hunting animals. He looked silly in the tall grass with a gun, hiding from nothing.

It only took a couple of hours to realize the

Oregon Trail was boring. There was nothing to do but walk. In spots, I could see ruts from the wagons that had gone before us. I wondered if there were children on those journeys, and if they were as bored as I was.

Finally we stopped. Mr. Lee walked down the line of wagons. He paused at each one and said, "Everyone all right?" People nodded, and he moved on to the next wagon. Mr. Adams stared at us the whole time.

I was glad when Mr. Lee announced we were done for the day and could settle in for dinner. We all ate next to our wagons and didn't mingle with the others. The only people Mama seemed to trust were Mr. Tucker and Charlie. I thought it was because of the voting and what Mr. Adams had said.

Suddenly Daddy stood up and said, "This doesn't make any sense. Everybody's suspicious of everybody else."

Daddy walked over to Mr. Tucker's wagon with James and his gun right behind him. When they came back, Mr. Tucker and Charlie were with them.

"Go on and sit down," said Daddy. "I'll be right back."

Daddy marched right up to Mr. Lee and his family. Daddy said something, and Mr. Lee and his wife smiled. Their whole family stood up and headed our way with their food.

I grinned at Mr. Lee's daughter. It was my way of thanking her for helping me get across the river.

Daddy introduced Mama to Mr. Lee's wife. "Cora, this is my wife, Ada. Ada, this is Cora."

Mama smiled. "Nice to meet you."

We all sat on the ground for dinner. Mr. Tucker and Charlie ate beans and dried beef. We had bread Mama had fried in bacon grease. The Lee family ate pork and corn bread. Usually, Mama was the first one to try to feed somebody, but she didn't offer to share our food. I knew she was worried about making it last.

Nobody said anything, but the silence said plenty. We were nervous and uncomfortable. Mr. Adams was staring as usual, but now he wore a deep frown on his face.

Mr. Lee's daughter broke the silence. "My name's Mattie. What's yours?" she asked me.

"Sarah," I said. I didn't really know any white children, since we couldn't go to school with them. Plus, we lived in a small town where all our neighbors were Negro.

Mattie looked at my doll. I hadn't let go of her since we left home. "I like your doll," she said.

"Thank you," I said. "My grandmother made her for me." I missed Granny and Granddaddy already. They were probably eating dinner too. The house was probably quiet and sad. I hoped Mattie and I could be friends. Maybe then I wouldn't feel so homesick.

After dinner we all went back to our own wagons. Mama had me and James sleep under the wagon, because she said it was the safest spot. Daddy kept a fire going nearby. The ground was hard and cold, and I was glad I had my quilt with me. I wrapped it around myself and pretended Granny was giving me a hug.

The next day, we ate breakfast before the sun could wake all the way up. Everyone looked like they were still half asleep.

Mr. Lee stood up and yelled. "All right, let's get back on the trail!"

Mattie's little brother, whose name was William, said, "Back on the trail!"

The wagons stayed in a line, but each day a new wagon was supposed to take the lead. Mr. Adams was today's leader.

"Mama, can I walk with Mattie?" I asked. Since they were first yesterday, they were last today. I was glad they weren't near Mr. Adams.

She smiled at me. "Just be careful," she said.

William was only five, and he seemed even happier than I was to be together. He ran in circles around us and sang songs. I thought we might have fun after all.

The oxen's feet and the wagon wheels kicked up a cloud of dust, but Mama had a little smile on her face as we continued. She and Daddy talked quietly, and I even heard him chuckle. Mattie sang a song, and I made my doll dance to the tune. It felt like Mattie and I had been friends all along.

Eating dinner together had changed something. At lunch Mr. Tucker sat in the grass, and my family joined him like it was the most natural thing in the world. Mr. Lee's family came over next. Eventually the man traveling with his wife

and mother joined us too. His name was Nicholas Carter, and his wife was Hannah. The older woman introduced herself. "I'm Nicholas's mother. You can call me Miss Edith."

Mr. Carter told us they were going to California to join family that had been there for two years. It gave me hope that maybe Granny and Granddaddy would join us after all.

The Edwards brothers and Mr. Adams must have been curious about our conversation. They came over and sat a bit further away than everyone else.

"We're not in Iowa anymore," said Young Mr. Edwards. "We're not in a state at all. This is Indian Territory."

Mr. Lee nodded.

Mr. Tucker said, "I heard they've killed a lot of people heading west."

"Killed people?" asked William. Mattie and I exchanged worried glances.

"Don't you worry." Mr. Adams held his gun up and shook it. "I'll shoot an Indian on sight if I have to."

Daddy stared Mr. Adams straight in the eye. "I don't think that'll be necessary."

"We'll see about that." Mr. Adams nodded at the others.

Daddy came right back with, "They were here first. This is their home."

I didn't know who was right. I'd heard stories about Indians attacking people on the trail, but they were always told by people who had never been on the trail. Once I heard a man say you were more likely to die in a wagon accident than to get killed by an Indian.

I knew one thing: We were bound to meet some Indians along the way. And as far as I could figure, *somebody* was going to end up hurt. Daddy wouldn't let Mr. Adams shoot someone for no reason. And Mr. Adams wouldn't let Daddy get away with trying to stop him.

Miss Edith said, "I remember the Black Hawk War. They got pushed right off their land. I'd be mad too."

"That's right," said Daddy. "Too many people are quick to judge and quick to kill." He looked at Mr. Adams when he said it, and everyone fell quiet.

CHAPTER FIVE

The Great Plains (Present Day Nebraska)
May 13, 1851

Mattie made the trip a lot more fun. We fetched water for the oxen together, ate together, and walked together. Sometimes we collected rocks and tried to see who could throw them the farthest. When there were clouds, we looked for shapes in the sky.

We reached Fort Kearny without running into any Indians. Fort Kearny was next to the Platte River, and it had a post office. While the adults bought supplies and rested, Mattie and I wrote letters home. I told Granny and Granddaddy all about the people, and crossing the river. I asked them some questions too, but I didn't know if I'd ever get the answers. How could they send me a letter if I didn't live anywhere?

Mattie wrote to her old best friend. When she finished, she looked at me and said, "I think we should be best friends now."

I nodded. "I think so too."

Mr. Lee returned and said, "We'll continue along the Platte." He paused and looked at each of us. "Then we'll have to cross."

The last thing I wanted to do was cross another river. Mattie must have known, because she took my hand and squeezed it.

That night, Mr. Adams took out his fiddle and played. The fiddle seemed like it was the only good thing about Mr. Adams, and whenever he played the mood was light. Those who slept in tents set up for the night. Those who slept out in the open, like Mama and Daddy, swatted at bugs and kept their eyes open for snakes. I think they were watching out for strangers too.

The next morning, we got up and went through what had become our normal routine. The women cooked breakfast. Sometimes it was flat biscuits fried in grease. Sometimes it was bacon or pancakes. It was *always* coffee. Everyone drank it. Even Mattie and I started drinking coffee. It didn't taste very good, but it was nice to start the day with something warm.

James had finally relaxed and stopped carrying his gun all over the place. "Dad," he said. "How will we get across the river?"

Daddy shook his head. "I'm not sure, son. I guess we'll figure that out when the time comes."

And soon enough, it was time to cross. As we got close to our crossing point, I could see a few people standing at the shore. When we were closer still, I saw they had light brown skin and dark, straight hair. I wondered if they were Indians. Mr. Edwards was leading us, and he brought his wagon to a stop. One by one, the wagons halted.

All my worries about the river turned into worries about the Indians, Mr. Adams, and Daddy.

Mr. Adams grabbed his gun and marched to the front of the wagon train. Daddy took his gun and followed right behind Mr. Adams. James tried to follow, but Mama held on to his arm. We all crept close enough to see and hear, but tried to take cover behind the wagons at the same time. I held Mama's hand. Mattie and William ran to their mama.

Without saying a word to the men on the shore, Mr. Adams aimed his gun at them.

"Lower your gun," said Daddy.

Mr. Adams spit on the ground. "You better stay out of this," he said. "I don't want to have to shoot you too."

“You’re not shooting at these men,” said Daddy. “They haven’t done anything to you.”

One of the Indians shouted at us, but we couldn’t make out what he said. Mr. Adams aimed at the one who had spoken. Before I could blink, Daddy had stepped into the line of fire.

“Theo!” Mama yelled. “Get out of the way! He’ll shoot you.”

Mr. Adams laughed. “You better listen to your wife, Lewis.”

Daddy ignored them both and stayed in between Mr. Adams and the Indians. Mama grabbed me and hugged me tight. She shoved my face into the front of her dress, so I couldn’t see what was about to happen. All I could do was listen and pray.

Mr. Lee said, “Mr. Adams, there’s no need to do anything rash.”

There was a long silence. I didn’t know who was going to die—Daddy, Mr. Adams, or one of the

Indian men. I heard shuffling, and I pulled away from Mama just in time to see Mr. Adams look through the sight of his gun, ready to shoot. Daddy lunged at him, which made the gun aim into the sky, and a shot went off. Everyone gasped. Mr. Lee grabbed the gun from Mr. Adams, and Daddy wrestled him to the ground.

"That was a mistake," Mr. Lee told Mr. Adams. "We might all be about to get killed." He convinced Mr. Adams to move behind everyone else.

Daddy kept his gun pointed away from the Indians and approached them slowly. They made no threatening moves but also showed no signs that they wanted to be friends. Daddy spoke to them, and there was a lot of gesturing, but I couldn't hear what they were saying. I wasn't even sure if they understood each other. I hoped the men realized Daddy was on their side.

After what felt like hours, Daddy returned to

the group. “They can take us across the river on their raft,” he said to Mr. Lee. “But we have to pay.”

Mr. Lee breathed a sigh of relief. “What do they want?”

“A gun,” said Daddy.

“I can’t say I blame them,” said Mr. Tucker.

Everyone looked at each other. It was obvious nobody wanted to give up their gun. Finally Daddy said, “James, give me your gun.”

“My gun?” asked James. “Granddaddy gave me this gun.” James looked like he might cry.

“Just give it to him, James,” said Mama.

James handed Daddy the gun and walked away with tears in his eyes. I felt bad for him. I knew it was partly about Granddaddy and partly because now he was back to being a boy.

Daddy walked back to the men on the shore. He gave them his own gun and kept the one from Granddaddy. Then he motioned for all of us to bring our wagons closer. The raft was small, so we had to cross the river one wagon at a time.

This time we went first. Since I'd done it once, I was a little less scared, but the water was freezing and the current was fast. I stayed as close to the middle of the raft as I could. I didn't believe the raft could support the weight of the wagon, but we made it across.

Once we were on land again and the raft was headed back, I heard Mama whisper, "Theo, you almost got yourself killed back there."

"Ada, I had to do something," said Daddy. "They aren't that different from us. Our people got stolen from home, and their home got stolen from them."

Mama sighed like she was more tired than she'd ever been.

It took most of the day to cross all of us, and Mr. Adams was last. I wondered if the Indians would throw Mr. Adams off the raft, but they didn't. If they had, I wouldn't have been very sad.

After the incident with the Indians, Mr. Adams seemed angry at all of us, and I could tell some of us didn't trust him. The Edwards brothers didn't seem bothered at all by Mr. Adams's behavior. Mr. Carter acted like he was on Mr. Adams's side too. I wasn't surprised, since they had voted for Mr. Adams to be the captain. I couldn't tell what some of the others thought.

We didn't have any more campfires with the whole party together. All that mattered to me was that my parents and Mattie's were still friends.

Most nights, there were at least three fires going. Mr. Adams and the Edwards brothers were always together. Our family, Mr. Lee's family, and Mr. Tucker and Charlie were often together. The Carter family kept to themselves. I had a feeling

Mr. Carter and his mother didn't see eye to eye on what happened at the Platte River.

One day at the end of May, Mr. Lee shouted, "We made it to Chimney Rock!"

It looked like a big mountain with a chimney growing out of the top. The most exciting thing about Chimney Rock was that it meant we weren't lost.

I sat in the shade of our wagon while some of the others admired Chimney Rock. Mr. Adams didn't know I could hear him when he said, "I can't stand Lewis. I should have shot him when I had the chance. I need to put him in his place."

"Yes, you do," said Mr. Edwards.

I'd like to see you try, I thought. Daddy had already wrestled him down once, and I knew he could do it again.

CHAPTER SIX

The Great Plains (Present Day Wyoming)
June 7, 1851

As we traveled beyond Chimney Rock, I noticed more evidence of the wagon trains that had headed west before us. There were broken wagon pieces, abandoned stoves, and even wagons that had been burned.

But the worst thing of all was the graves. Every time we passed a cluster of buried travelers, I wanted to cry. I wondered who they were and what had happened to them. I tried to imagine what it would be like if one of us didn't make it. Would we go on without them? Would we turn back for home?

"Mama," I asked, "why are there so many graves?"

Mama sighed. "Lots of reasons. Starvation. Accidents. Cholera."

"What's cholera?" I asked.

Mattie chimed in. "I've heard of it. It's a sickness. My mother said one day you're fine, and the next day you're dead."

I looked at Mama to see if Mattie was right. "It's killed a lot of people," Mama said.

"I hope we don't get it," I said. I waited for Mama to promise me we'd be okay, but she didn't.

It felt like the days were getting longer. I was tired of walking. I was tired of eating hard bread and beans. I was tired of keeping an eye on Mr. Adams all the time. Sometimes I would catch him looking at Daddy. Then he would see me watching and look away.

We had less fun as the time passed. One of

the Edwards's oxen died, and Mama's feet were swollen. She wrapped them in cloth for extra padding, but she was limping. Mr. Carter's mother barely said a word lately, and Mr. Tucker and Daddy often whispered to each other.

James and Charlie had struck up a friendship, just like Mattie and I had. They ate together at meals and entertained themselves throwing stones at different targets.

It was starting to feel like we'd be on the trail for the rest of our lives.

Fort Laramie (Present Day Wyoming)
June 10, 1851

William exclaimed, "Look!" He pointed in the opposite direction from where I had been looking.

"We've reached Fort Laramie!" Mr. Lee shouted. Cheers rang out, and the pace picked up some.

Daddy said, "That means we're getting closer to the halfway point. We'll be at Independence Rock in no time."

Fort Laramie was much better than Fort Kearny. It was the closest thing to a town I'd seen in a long time. It had three bakeries, a blacksmith, and a wagon maker's shop. Daddy gave me and James some money for the bakery, and Mattie came with us. We got fresh loaves of warm bread. It was a welcome change from the flat, crunchy bread made out of flour and boiled water that had come from the river.

One evening, a few days after we left the fort, Mr. Tucker, Charlie, and James shot several squirrels. Mr. Tucker cooked them. Even though it tasted good, I didn't eat it all. I felt too guilty eating a cute little squirrel.

"I brought you a treat," said Mattie.

"What is it?" I asked.

Mattie grinned. "Open your hand and close your eyes."

I did what she said and felt her press something into my palm. It was a piece of dried fruit. I missed sweets. Granny used to bake pies all the time, and there was no such thing as dessert on the Oregon Trail.

I popped it in my mouth and let the sweetness cover my whole tongue. Then I hugged Mattie. "Thank you." She was the best friend I'd ever had.

The day we arrived at Independence Rock, I had been walking with Mama, because she was tired and sore. Mr. Lee's wagon was back at the end of the train, so Mattie and William had been a few wagons behind us all day.

Mr. Adams, who was in the lead, shouted, "Independence Rock! We're halfway there!"

Mr. Carter said, "Good, we can rest. My mother isn't feeling well."

"What's wrong?" asked Mrs. Lee.

"I think she's dehydrated," said Mr. Carter. "And her stomach is a little upset."

Mama and I looked at each other. She had told me those were signs of cholera. I hoped it was just old age.

Independence Rock wasn't much to look at—just a mound of stone growing out of the nothingness. Once we were close enough, I could see that travelers had carved their names in the rock. I ran to find Mattie so we could add our names together. She wasn't with her family. I went from wagon to wagon, but I couldn't find her anywhere.

Finally I went to her father. "Where is Mattie?" I asked.

"That girl," said Mr. Lee. "I bet she ran off to the rock."

"No, she didn't," said William. "She's playing in the grass."

Mattie's mother walked back to get her. I was too excited to wait, so I carved *S-A-R-A-H* into the rock.

At dinnertime, Mrs. Lee returned without Mattie. "I can't find her anywhere," she said. She was out of breath, and her face was pink.

Before any of us could answer, a loud wail came from the Carters' wagon. We ran to see what happened. Mrs. Carter was in the wagon, holding the limp body of Mr. Carter's mother. She looked at us with tears streaming down her face. "She's dead."

Independence Rock had turned out to be Disaster Rock. Mr. Carter dug a grave for his mother while the rest of us went back and forth between grief and hoping none of us got cholera. We had a sad little funeral for her. Mr. Carter sobbed. I didn't know what I'd do if my mama died.

Mattie's family didn't come to the funeral. They whispered to each other over by their wagon. Finally Mr. Lee decided to search for Mattie.

"Can I go?" I asked.

"Absolutely not," said Mama.

Daddy shook his head. "The last thing we need is two missing girls."

I frowned and thought, *A woman can do anything a man can do.*

Mr. Adams joined us. "A delay might cause us to end up stuck in the mountains in the middle of winter. Then we'll *all* be missing."

We all stared at him. A girl was missing, and that was more important than anything else.

Finally Mr. Lee said, "He's right. If I'm not back by morning, you need to leave without me."

"We're not letting you go alone," said Mr. Tucker. "Lewis and I will come with you. We can cover more ground."

"I'll come too," said James.

Daddy put his hands on James's shoulders. "Son," he said. "I need you to stay here. Take care of your mama and sister." Daddy lowered his voice. "And keep your distance from the Carters. They might be sick."

Understanding spread across James's face, and he gave Daddy a serious nod. Maybe James wanted to stay, but I didn't. With Miss Edith dead, three men leaving, and my best friend missing, we could end up with *five* people gone for good.

I watched the three men leave on foot, through the tall grass to find Mattie. Then, when no one was paying attention, I snuck off after them.

CHAPTER SEVEN

Just east of Independence Rock (Present Day Wyoming)
June 22, 1851

I stayed hidden in the tall grass. I kept Daddy in sight, because he was the tallest and easy to see.

Mr. Lee said, "I don't know how we left her behind like this." He sounded like he was crying.

"You know how kids are," said Mr. Tucker. "They're always doing something they shouldn't be."

Daddy agreed. "Yeah, it's not your fault."

The three men called for Mattie, and every time I listened for her answer. It never came. When the sun went down, they split up to cover more ground. If they didn't find Mattie soon, we might have to sleep out here. I didn't want to sleep alone in the grass.

Their yells got more worried as the night went on. I decided not to stay right behind them anymore. I was just looking where they were looking. If I wanted to find my friend, I needed to look where they didn't.

They were on the side of the trail where we rested

earlier. I crossed over to the other side. I wanted to call out to Mattie, but I'd give myself away. I walked in a zigzag pattern, so I wouldn't miss any spots, but didn't get too far away.

Daddy's voice sounded farther away the next time he called Mattie's name, and I knew we were going in opposite directions. I stood still and thought, *What would I do if I got left behind?*

We had eaten while we rested, so I didn't think Mattie would have looked for food. If I were her, I would have stayed right where I was so people could find me. Mattie might have decided to try to find us when the sun went down.

Then I knew what she would have done. She would have followed the ruts from the wagon wheels. I wondered if she knew which way to go. If she had been walking around, she could have gotten confused. *Not Mattie,* I thought. *She would have gone the right way.*

I headed back the way we came, but I walked in between the ruts. I could still hear the men calling, and they were the same distance away as before.

"Mattie?" I whispered very quietly, hoping she could hear me but the men couldn't. She didn't answer me, but I crept along whispering her name.

My eyes had adjusted to the dark, so I looked from side to side. Mattie had worn a white dress. At least, it used to be white. We were all filthy. There were no warm baths on the trail—just dips in the river. The dirty white dress would still be easy to spot in the dark, though.

There was a rustling sound in the grass to my left. I crouched and waited. For the first time, I was scared. It could be a snake or some other dangerous animal. I stayed close to the ground and listened. I didn't hear anything else—not even the voices of the men. It was like I was out there all alone.

The rustle came again from further away.

Whatever it was hadn't seen me.

Oh no! I thought. *What if it was Mattie?* Mattie could have thought she heard a person and come closer. I had stayed quiet and still, so she might be walking away.

I knew it could be a deadly mistake, but I walked into the grass where the sound had come from. I heard it again and followed. It got louder but seemed to be running away from me. Maybe it was scared.

"Mattie?" I whispered.

The rustling stopped.

"Mattie?" I repeated. Something was telling me to go toward the sound. I took another step. The thing in the grass didn't move.

"Mattie?" This time I said it louder.

There was a loud stirring in the grass. It sounded too big to be Mattie. It was rushing toward me. I dropped to the ground, curled into a ball, and covered my head with my hands.

CHAPTER EIGHT

Independence Rock
June 22, 1851

"Sarah?"

It *was* Mattie. I laughed and stood up. Mattie threw her arms around me. "You scared me!" I said.

"*You* scared *me.*" Mattie giggled. "I'm glad you found me."

"You didn't hear your father calling you?" I asked.

Mattie shook her head. "I walked for a long time, but I sat down to rest," she said. "I accidentally fell asleep. I just woke up."

Mattie and I locked elbows and made our way to the ruts. When we came out of the grass, a man was headed toward us. I recognized Daddy, even in the dark. When he got closer, he recognized us too.

"Sarah?" Daddy sounded shocked. "Mattie?"

I wanted to run to Daddy, but I knew I was in trouble. He started yelling. "Lee! Lee! She's here!"

Daddy ran to us, lifted us both up at the same time, and squeezed us tight. "Thank God," he whispered.

Mr. Lee and Mr. Tucker came running. Mr. Lee took Mattie from Daddy's arms and hugged her.

Daddy put me down. "Sarah," he said, "I told you to stay put. You could have gotten lost. Or worse."

"Lewis." Mr. Lee's voice was quiet. "She may have saved Mattie's life."

Daddy frowned. He stared at me for a long time and then he burst into laughter. "Let's get back to our camp," he said.

By the time we returned, it was daylight. Mr. Carter's wagon was coming toward us.

"What's going on?" asked Mr. Lee when the wagon stopped.

Mr. Carter looked down. "We're going home."

Daddy said, "You're going back?"

Mr. Carter nodded. "We were hoping life in California would bring joy back to my mother. She hasn't been the same since my father died."

"She loved adventure," said Mrs. Carter. She started to cry.

"Good luck," said Mr. Tucker.

As they rode away, Mama, James, Charlie, Mrs. Lee, and William ran over to us. Mrs. Lee dropped to her knees and hugged Mattie.

Mama did the same to me. "Sarah, you didn't

have any business sneaking off like that," she scolded me.

"She's the one who found Mattie," Daddy told her.

They all looked at me. I could tell I wasn't in trouble after all.

James said, "There was trouble while you were gone."

"Mr. Adams declared himself the leader," said Charlie. "Since you all left, there was no one there to speak out against him."

"I tried," said James. "He wouldn't listen. He kept saying we were going to freeze to death in the mountains if we waited."

"Mr. Adams and the Edwards brothers left with our child missing," said Mrs. Lee. "First thing this morning." She sounded disgusted.

"Good riddance," said Daddy.

Charlie said, "Now it's just us our three families.

Traveling will be much harder with only three wagons."

"We had safety in our numbers," said James.

"Well, the best of us are still here," said Mr. Lee. "We'll make it."

Part of me believed Mr. Lee. The other part of me worried about taking too long and getting caught in the mountains during winter.

Mama made breakfast for all of us. I didn't realize I was starving until I smelled the pork cooking. Even the flat bread tasted good.

While we were eating, Mrs. Lee said, "Mattie, how did you get left behind in the first place?"

I had been so happy to find my friend I hadn't even thought to ask what happened. Mattie looked embarrassed and didn't answer right away.

Mama said, "It's okay. Whatever it is, don't be ashamed."

Mattie sighed and said, "I had to go to the

bathroom. I needed some privacy, so I waited until everyone was packing up."

I giggled, and Mama shot me a look, so I stopped and let Mattie tell her story.

"I wandered off too far and got lost," said Mattie. "By the time I found my way back, you were gone."

I covered my mouth so I wouldn't laugh. Mattie looked at me, and a great big smile spread across her face.

"Stop laughing," she said, even though she was laughing too. It was good to have my friend back safe and sound.

We packed up our wagons just like we had every other morning. Mr. Lee told us we'd be heading toward the Rocky Mountains next. Since I wasn't usually next to Mr. Lee, I had never noticed that he had a book of notes and a rough map he was following. I was glad we had directions.

Mr. Lee handed the paper to Daddy. "Lewis, why don't you lead for a while? I'd like to tend to my family."

Daddy took the paper and nodded. "I wonder if we'll catch up with Adams and the Edwards brothers."

Mr. Tucker answered, "I hope not."

Even though our wagon train was a lot smaller now, the mood was lighter. Now it felt like a group of friends—or maybe even family. We talked as we traveled. Sometimes Mama and Mrs. Lee joined in when Mattie and I sang songs. Our days fell into a rhythm that felt easy.

Eventually, we could see a mountain range in the distance.

As we looked toward the mountains, a figure headed toward us. Since we outnumbered him, we continued forward, but with caution.

As the captain, it was Daddy's job to approach

the person. "Stop here," said Daddy. "I'll talk to him alone."

"I'll come with you," said Mr. Tucker.

Daddy's forehead creased. "We can't spare any men."

Mr. Tucker nodded and stayed with Charlie. I held my breath as Daddy approached the stranger. After a short conversation, Daddy motioned us forward.

"He explained how to find South Pass. He also knows a shortcut once we're through the mountains," said Daddy. "It's called the Hastings Cutoff."

I looked at the man in front of us. He looked like he'd been living in the mountains his whole life. He was hairy and wore fur clothing. He was dirty, too, but by now, so were all of us. After he gave Daddy directions, Mama gave the man some beans and bread, and he went on his way.

The trip through the mountains was slow and a lot bumpier than the plains had been, but they were pretty. I was glad to have something to look at other than grass. The trees were taller and greener, and there were more birds. Mattie and I tried to count the different kinds of birds to make the trip go faster, and eventually, we came out on the other side.

West of the Rocky Mountains
August 6, 1851

In the distance, we could see another fort. It was made out of adobe, and several wagons were loading up to leave. Our weary bodies were ready for a break, so we were happy, but Daddy looked concerned. He didn't say anything, but he looked at his map a few too many times. He was making me nervous.

When Daddy saw we were at a place called Fort Hall, he mumbled under his breath.

"What's wrong, Theo?" asked Mr. Tucker.

Daddy frowned at the map. "This isn't right. We're too far north."

"I'll go inside and talk to someone," said Mr. Lee. We all waited with our wagons while Mr. Lee went inside the fort. When he returned, he said, "I have bad news."

We gathered around to hear whatever Mr. Lee had learned. "We missed the Hastings Cutoff," he said. "We missed the California branch of the trail altogether."

I knew Daddy didn't do it on purpose, but I was upset. I didn't want to spend any more time on the trail than we had to.

"I knew it," said Daddy. He looked at all of us, then hung his head. "I'm sorry. We're off track by weeks."

"Yes, we are," said Mr. Lee. "But you also might have saved our lives. The man I talked to said the Hastings Cutoff is no good."

"No good?" asked Mr. Tucker. "What's wrong with it?"

"There's no water for about ninety miles." Mr. Lee chuckled. "You may have done us a favor, Lewis."

Even though we were lucky not to be on the Hastings Cutoff, we had gone miles out of our way.

"We've lost some time," said Mr. Lee. "We need to beat winter. If we're stuck in the mountains past October, we'll be dealing with snow. We aren't prepared for that kind of weather, and we might have to leave the oxen and wagons behind."

That didn't sound good at all. We'd freeze to death if we got stuck in the mountains.

"The other thing is," said Mr. Lee, "during the winter storms it's hard to see, and we could get lost." There was only one thing to do. Go faster.

Our hearts were heavy as we unloaded all the extra weight from our wagons. We left behind tools we wouldn't need until we got to California. We dumped everything from our heavy trunks into the wagon and tossed the trunks aside. Mr. Tucker and Charlie had to leave the farming equipment they'd brought with them.

Luckily, Daddy hadn't spent much money, so he bought some food to make sure we wouldn't run out. The oxen were able to move faster. As the weeks passed, we walked faster too, because the air was beginning to cool off. That only meant one thing. Winter was approaching.

The fun we'd had going from Independence Rock to Fort Hall was long gone. Mr. Lee and Daddy walked with the front wagon and kept the pace. They wore serious expressions and didn't talk much.

The women, girls, and William walked next to the second wagon. Mr. Lee wanted to make sure no more children got lost, and he figured two mothers watching us was better than one. We didn't sing anymore, because we were saving our breath. It wasn't easy keeping up with Daddy and Mr. Lee all day.

Mr. Tucker, James, and Charlie brought up the rear, and that part bothered me the most. I knew Mr. Lee and Daddy were trying to protect us by keeping us in the middle, but all it did was remind me that we were heading into more dangerous territory—and maybe winter—soon.

CHAPTER NINE

East of the Sierra Nevada Mountains
September 23, 1851

We all had mixed feelings as we stood looking at the Sierra Nevada Mountains way off in the distance. We were close to California. But this last portion of the trip was the most dangerous. I kept imagining our wagons stuck in the snow and all of us walking along a cliff through a blizzard.

"Let's set up camp for tonight and start fresh in the morning," said Daddy.

That was fine with me. I needed time to prepare myself for the mountains. It was going to take a lot of courage.

We sat around the campfire and ate a good dinner. Charlie and James had gone hunting and came back with a few squirrels. This time I was glad to have them. We had beans, and Mattie's family shared some of their dried fruit. The men shared some of the stories they had heard about the mountains.

Mr. Lee said, "Have you heard about the Donners?"

Mr. Tucker and Charlie nodded. My family had never heard of them, so Mr. Lee continued. "They got stuck in these mountains in the middle of winter. Almost all of them died."

When Mr. Lee finished, the only sound was the fire. Mattie and I huddled together. We were about to head into those same mountains, just a little bit closer to winter than we'd hoped. I wished Mr. Lee hadn't told us about the Donners.

At Fort Hall, Mr. Lee had been given a tip to use the Beckwourth Pass. We were lucky enough to find the path early in October, and even saw evidence that a wagon train had recently traveled through. Remains of campfires still looked fresh, and there were still ruts from wagon wheels.

The pass had ups and downs. The air got colder, and we had to wear several layers of clothes to stay warm. That made it harder to walk, but we didn't have a choice. I wondered how much longer this part of the trip would be.

West of the Beckwourth Pass, Sierra Nevada Mountains
October 17, 1851

Then one morning it happened. We'd only been traveling for a few hours after breakfast when the first snow fell. It was just a light snow, and it didn't even stick to the ground, but it was still snow.

"We need to pick up the pace," said Mr. Lee.

Mattie whispered, "He's worried."

"I am too," I whispered back.

We took shorter breaks and traveled for an extra hour each day. The nights were freezing, and we built bigger fires to stay warm. I sat with my doll, wrapped up in the quilt Granny made. It reminded me of the night I found out Daddy was taking this trip. I wished I was home in my own bed.

A few days later, enough snow fell to cover the ground. We went as fast as we could, determined to make it to California before the worst of it hit. Later in the day, we got to a downward slope.

We all stood at the top and looked down. It was too steep for the wagons. I hoped we wouldn't have to leave them behind. I didn't want our poor oxen to die in the snow.

The men decided it was best to chop some small logs to put in front of the wheels. They said it would help slow the wagons down.

All of us took turns chopping, even me and Mattie. I liked helping, because all that chopping warmed me up. By evening, we had enough logs. We unhitched the oxen, so that if the wagons went out of control, they wouldn't be stuck to them. Mr. Lee led his wagon down first, then Mr. Tucker. Even though they had to work to keep the wagons straight, they made it down.

I was glad I'd watched the first two wagons, because I was less worried about ours now. Our wagon was doing fine, but somehow one of the logs slipped. There was a popping sound, and the wagon lurched forward. The log had cracked.

The log moved again, and the wagon jerked to a stop.

"James, get another log!" yelled Daddy.

I ran with James and helped him carry it. "Where should I put it?" he asked.

"We're going to have to do two things at once," said Daddy. "We have to move the cracked one, and slide the new one in."

I moved out of the way. I didn't understand how he was going to put the new one in place if the other one was still right there. It seemed like as soon as he moved the cracked one, the wagon would roll.

Daddy looked at James. "I'll count to three. Ready?"

James nodded.

"One . . . two . . . three!" Daddy yelled. Daddy pulled the bad log, but before James could get the new one in place, the wagon started down the hill.

I gasped as it picked up too much speed. It flew down the hill toward our friends at the bottom.

"Mattie!" I yelled. I didn't want the wagon to run her over.

"Everybody move!" Daddy hollered.

The wagon continued to pick up speed as our friends scattered and screamed, and all I could do was watch through my tears.

CHAPTER TEN

Sierra Nevada Mountains
October 20, 1851

Mr. Lee's family, Mr. Tucker, and Charlie got out of the way just before our wagon crashed into a tree. The front of the wagon broke, and a wheel fell off.

"Oh no!" cried Mama. "Now what?"

"We leave it," said Daddy. He made his way to the bottom of the slope with me, Mama, and James trailing behind him. We stopped when we got to our destroyed wagon.

"What about all of our things?" I asked.

Mr. Tucker and Charlie immediately began

taking things from our wagon and putting them into their own. Mr. Lee joined in, and between the three of them, they moved all the food and clothes.

Next, Mama and I climbed into the wagon and found our little wooden treasure boxes. Granddaddy had made them for us one Christmas. Mama's held a locket from her mother, who had died when Mama was very young. In mine, I kept a pair of tiny wooden birds Granddaddy had carved for me.

Mrs. Lee and Mattie stood at the back of the wagon with their arms stretched toward us. We handed them our boxes, and they carefully cradled them in their hands as we climbed out. Even though I was starting to hate the Oregon Trail, my heart was filled with love for our friends.

We hooked two of our oxen to Mr. Tucker's wagon, and walked the other two next to us. We had to leave some things behind, but I knew we had what was most important—each other.

Coloma, California
November 1, 1851

We made our way through the mountains only to find another stretch of land in front of us. Just when I thought we'd never make it, I saw smoke rising into the air. I took Mattie's hand and squeezed it.

"That's it. It has to be," I whispered. "We made it all the way to California." I was suddenly filled with curiosity about a place I hadn't even wanted to come to.

Daddy wrapped Mama in his arms and hugged her for a long time. She cried into his coat. "We made it," she said.

When we made it into the town of Coloma, the scene in front of us was like nothing I'd ever seen.

All kinds of people lived there—old, young, and people of different races. As we walked, we passed a post office, stores run by Chinese people, and what looked like hundreds of miners along the river in tents and cabins. Most of them were men.

T OFFICE

California was loud and dirty and crowded. Nobody looked like they had struck it rich. Some of the people looked too thin. It was nothing like home, and I couldn't imagine a life for us here. We must have looked like we were in shock.

A Negro woman approached us and said, "Do you need some help?"

Mama looked relieved. "We have no idea what to do now that we're here," she said.

The woman stuck out her hand. "I'm Mrs. Nancy Gooch."

"I'm Ada." Mama introduced Mrs. Gooch to all of us. "Have you been here long?"

"Almost two years. It's not as bad as it looks," Mrs. Gooch said. "Come on, I'll show you around."

Mrs. Gooch pointed out a gun shop and a few homes. She seemed happy, and it gave me hope that we could be happy too.

"Did you leave home to be a miner?" asked Mama.

Mrs. Gooch made a sound with her mouth. "No. I was brought here as a slave. In 1850, California became a free state, so I got my freedom."

Daddy said, "And you stayed here?"

"Wasn't anything else to do," she said. "Me and my husband figured we'd go on and make our life here. I tell you what, though. The money isn't in the river."

"What do you mean?" asked James. He leaned in like he was about to hear a secret.

"These miners are mostly men. They're away from home, and a lot of them can't do a thing for themselves." Mrs. Gooch winked. "You can make a lot more money cleaning, sewing, and selling homemade food."

James looked disappointed. Mama and Daddy looked at each other. I could tell they didn't know what to think.

I didn't know what to think. Daddy brought

us here for a better life, but I wasn't sure if this was better.

"But there *is* gold, right?" asked James.

"There is," said Mrs. Gooch. "You'll be okay."

I could tell everyone was relieved. Daddy said, "Ada, if I mine for gold, and you cook up some of your good food, we could really do well." He sounded excited all over again.

That night we set up camp as far away from the crowd as we could. We could hear men laughing and yelling. Mama and Daddy had already started planning.

"Do you think we'll stay?" asked Mama.

Daddy nodded. "At least for a while. There are choices here. We can earn money and go back if we need to," he said. "That was the original plan anyway."

"Or maybe we can stay and save, then find a quieter spot to live," said Mama. The tiniest bit of excitement snuck into her voice.

Mattie leaned close to me and whispered in my ear. "We should learn to make biscuits and sell them to the miners."

I grinned and nodded. If all of us pitched in, we really could make a good living. I took out a piece of paper and a pen.

Dear Granny and Granddaddy,

We made it to California. This is our first night here, in a place called Coloma. I don't know if I'm going to like it, but at least our whole family survived. A woman here said the miners will pay high prices for the things they miss from home. My friend Mattie and I are going to sell biscuits to the miners so we can earn money. I already know what we'll call them: Golden Biscuits!

Love,
Sarah

That night I fell asleep smiling. I liked the idea of helping my family. Plus, I had my new best friend. *Maybe a different life won't be so bad after all,* I thought.

A NOTE FROM THE AUTHOR

When I write historical fiction it's important to me that I tell as accurate a story as possible. I also try to show points of view that aren't always shown when these histories are told. This story made that challenging.

I wanted to tell the story from the perspective of an African American girl. We don't always get to read about the many African Americans who made the trip west. I also wanted to show that the trip was difficult for those traveling the Oregon Trail. Perhaps most importantly, I wanted to make sure I showed that "Westward Expansion" was tragic for those who were already there: the Native American people.

The west was not a "frontier." It was not new or unknown. American Indians suffered greatly because of Europeans and the California Gold Rush. Native Americans across the country were forced off their homelands and killed in battles over their land. Their cultures and histories were disregarded. Their way of life was completely disrupted.

Sarah's journey ends in Coloma, California. Before

the arrival of Europeans, this land was home to the Nisenan, Maidu, and Miwok Indians. American Indians were discriminated against and used as slave labor. They were exposed to deadly diseases and were devastated by the Gold Rush.

About 300,000 Native Americans lived in California before Europeans arrived. By 1860, there were fewer than 30,000. Despite this, Native American culture has survived and thrived. Many American Indians are still very much in touch with their heritage today.

I chose to use my characters' actions and words to show the varying perspectives that people during this time held. I hope you noticed greed, ignorance, and fear. I also hope you recognized empathy, hope, and people who spoke up. If I have done my job, this book is honest, sensitive, and respectful. I'm grateful to my friends and colleagues who helped me work toward my goals for this book.

In *Sarah Journeys West*, Sarah's family's "jumping off point" is Kanesville, Iowa. It was renamed Council Bluffs in 1853. This was a popular spot for those beginning their journey. Another popular jumping off point was Independence, Missouri. Sarah's family left from Iowa, because at the time this story takes place, Missouri was a slave state. It would not have been as realistic to have them living there.

The places through which Sarah traveled are real places. Many of the landmarks can still be visited today. Beckwourth Pass is named for James Beckwourth (1798–1866). He was an African American man born into slavery in Virginia. He was freed and eventually headed west. He was a blacksmith, explorer, trapper, "mountain man," and military scout. The pass was already well-traveled by Native Americans. James Beckwourth cleared and improved the trail.

Beckwourth was also apparently quite a storyteller. In one of his stories, he claims he was captured by the Crow Indians who thought he was the son of a chief. He was then reportedly let into the tribe and married a chief's daughter. It's said that he lived with the tribe for six years, became a war chief, and led raids against other tribes. Even though he exaggerated, many of Beckwourth's stories are rooted in truth. James Beckwourth recorded his own life history, which was published in 1856. It was titled *The Life and Adventures of James P. Beckwourth.*

Nancy Gooch, who helps Sarah's family get settled in Coloma, is based on a real person. Nancy Ross Gooch (1811–1901) and her husband Peter were brought to Coloma as slaves. They became free after the Compromise of 1850 made California a "free state." Nancy had to leave her son behind when she was brought to California. She earned money to buy his freedom by washing and mending clothes and cooking. By 1858, she owned eighty acres of land. Eventually her family owned nearly four hundred acres.

History is full of little-known people from diverse backgrounds who accomplished amazing things. Many of them were women. I'm thankful that I get to play a small part in telling those stories, and I hope you enjoyed *Sarah Journeys West*.

GLOSSARY

appetite (AP-uh-tite)—desire for food

cholera (KAH-lur-uh)—a dangerous disease that causes severe vomiting and diarrhea, usually due to infected water

declare (dee-KLAIR)—to announce something formally

dehydrated (dee-HYE-dray-tid)—lacking enough water in your body for normal functioning

fiddle (FID-uhl)—a violin

homemade (HOME-mayd)—made at home or by hand

homesick (HOME-sik)—missing your home, family, and/or friends while you are away

incident (IN-si-dehnt)—an event

mine (MINE)—to dig up minerals that are in the ground

miracle (MIR-uh-kuhl)—a lucky event

rhythm (RITH-uhm)—a repeated pattern of movement or sound

slavery (SLAY-vuh-ree)—the practice of owning people and thinking of them as property

suspicious (suh-SPISH-uhs)—having or showing distrust of someone

MAKING CONNECTIONS

1. In the beginning of the story, Sarah does not want to make the journey west, but her parents make her come with them. Write a paragraph giving your opinion about this. Do you think Sarah should have been allowed to stay at home with Granny and Granddaddy? Why or why not?

2. In Chapter Five, Sarah's wagon train makes it to Fort Kearny, where she writes a letter home. Pretend you are Sarah, and write a letter to Granny and Granddaddy. Include events from the story, as well as Sarah's feelings and responses to those events.

3. Sarah's party realized they were heading in the wrong direction when they got to Fort Hall. They made the decision to turn around and get back onto the California Trail. Use the map to determine how their trip might have been different if they had continued on the Oregon Trail instead. Consider the terrain and their destination in your answer.

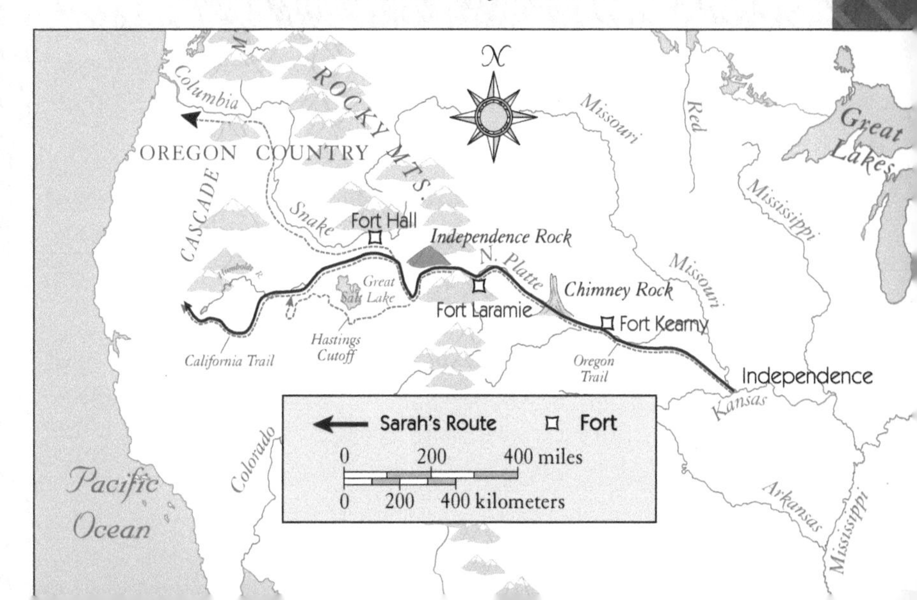

ABOUT THE AUTHOR

Nikki Shannon Smith is from Oakland, California, but she now lives in the Central Valley with her husband and two children. She has worked in elementary education for more than twenty-five years and writes everything from picture books to young adult novels. When she's not busy with family, work, or writing, she loves to visit the coast. The first thing she packs in her suitcase is always a book.